Bambi

Edited by Stella Croker

Longmeadow Press

One day, as the sun rose, there was great excitement in the forest. The first morning rays lightly touched the top of the big trees.

Deep in the forest, all the animals were awakening. Springtime had finally come and leaves were sprouting everywhere.

The squirrel who lived in the top of a big tree stretched and yawned. Mr Owl who had been hunting all night long, and who was very tired, hardly noticed the squirrel jumping from branch to branch.

"Hello Miss Mouse," said the squirrel to a little mouse, who was strolling by.

"Did you know it's springtime again?" she asked, with a happy smile on her face.

"Yes, it's lovely and in the blink of an eye, it'll be summer again, time for raspberry and strawberry picking," chattered the squirrel.

"And what about a little race to the big pine tree?" he continued.

As soon as they started running, they were joined by Thumper the rabbit.

"Quick, quick," twittered two flying birds, "hurry, hurry," repeated a group of rabbits that had suddenly popped out.

"He's been born. He's been born," they all sang.

"Who's been born?" asked the squirrel.

"The little fawn has been born: Bambi, the son of the great stag."

All the animals and birds went to welcome him. Flying, crawling, jumping, they were all there. Everyone wanted to see the little prince.

"Where is he? Where is he?" The fawn was still sleeping against his mother.

All the hustle and bustle hadn't awakened him yet.

Mother deer gave him a tender caress. The fawn opened his eyes and looked around.

"Here are all your friends," said his mother, "they've all come to see you and to say "hello"."

Thumper who was a daring little rabbit came closer and said: "We promise to be good with Bambi, we will all look after him." All the animals nodded their heads.

For a moment Bambi looked a little frightened, then he tried to stand. At first his legs wobbled, but soon he stood firmly and without shaking.

Thumper asked him "What is your name, little fawn?"
"Bambi," answered the fawn shyly.

"That's a pretty name," said the rabbit. "My name is
Thumper and I think we'll be good friends. I know a lot
of games, you see."

Everybody went back home to spread the news of the
new arrival, except Thumper who was impatient to play
with Bambi, but Bambi had already fallen asleep again.

Thumper could hardly wait for him to wake up so
they could start playing together.

"One, two, three, four, five, six."

Bambi was learning to count. Mrs Quail is teaching him and he repeats the numbers after her.

It's easy to count when each number has the shape of a little quail.

As Bambi got a little older, he loved to walk along the leafy paths of the forest, finding new surprises every day.

One day, he found some oppossums hanging upside down.

"How strange," he thought. He bent over to see how things looked from upside down, but he soon gave up because he was getting quite dizzy.

Sometimes Bambi played with Thumper, the rabbit, who showed him all sorts of new things and told him their names. "Those are birds," said Thumper and Bambi said "Birds." It was fun to see so many different things and to be able to give them a name.

When a butterfly came along, Bambi proudly called out "Bird, bird."

"No, that's not a bird," said Thumper with a big laugh. "Then it's a flower that flies," Bambi suggested.

"Flowers don't fly" replied Thumper. "What is it then?" Bambi asked, very puzzled.

"It is a butterfly." pronounced Thumper.

"It's very pretty. If I weren't a fawn, I would like to be a butterfly," declared Bambi. "It's wonderful to live here, with so many friends and so many things to discover!"

Bambi was a good student, he remembered everything he had been taught. One day he was playing in a field when something with a small black pointed nose popped up out of the flowers.

"Are you a rabbit?" Bambi asked.

"No, sir." "Are you a mouse?" he asked.

"No sir." "Are you a squirrel then? What are you? I've never seen anybody like you," Bambi continued.

"I'm a skunk," came the answer.

"Look at my beautiful fur," the skunk said.

"You do have a beautiful fur," replied Bambi, who couldn't help thinking that the skunk was bragging a little.

Thumper who happened to pass by, added "Your fur may be beautiful, but skunks stink," and burst into laughter.

"I didn't smell anything," said Bambi, "and his fur is beautiful." He didn't need to say any more. He had found a new friend.

The sun wasn't always shining in the forest.

"The forest is crying. Look, tears are falling on the leaves," Bambi said to his mother one day. His mother explained to him that it was raining.

"You see, it's only a big cloud up in the sky that has just burst and now thanks to the water, all the leaves will be greener and new flowers will grow and bloom."

Bambi wasn't the only one to wonder about the rain.
Up in their nest, the new-born birds had a bad
surprise when this unexpected shower started.

Fortunately, their mother spread her wings and it was
nice and warm underneath, like being under a big
umbrella. All the little birds went back to sleep to the
sound of the raindrops falling.

When the shower was over, everything looked brand new. The grass, the flowers, the bright leaves. Bambi jumped with pleasure. "Summer is coming," he shouted, bubbling with excitement.

One morning, Thumper came hopping along saying: "Bambi, I've discovered a wonderful place, let's go there together."

"My mother doesn't like me to go too far, she says it is dangerous for fawns."

"We won't stay long and besides, it's full of delicious things to eat." Thumper knew that Bambi wouldn't resist such an offer.

"Things to eat!" Bambi said, suddenly becoming interested.

"Well, let's go then, why are we wasting time?"

Both of them started running and Bambi thought he had never seen so many trees. It seemed as if the forest would never come to an end.

They finally arrived at the edge of a big meadow, which looked like a large carpet strewn with flowers.

"Here it is," Thumper proudly exclaimed, "time for a snack. All these pink flowers are delicious," he said biting one. "Why don't you do the same, Bambi?"

Both of them started eating with very big appetites.

"I will become the fattest rabbit in the forest and you will grow to be so tall that you will be able to reach the top of the trees," announced Thumper, disappearing into the carpet of flowers.

"I'm thirsty," said Bambi after a while.

"There is a puddle not far from here," Thumper said between mouthfuls.

Bambi was amazed how much his friend knew.

The two animals set out for this new destination.

Suddenly something sprang up out of the grass. Bambi startled, saw the green thing vanish into a pool of water.

"That's a frog. It lives near the water and we disturbed him, so that's why it's hiding," Thumper explained, "then, when we are gone, it will poke its head out of the water again and play hide-and-seek with the other frogs."

Bambi moved closer to the water's edge, but, as he bent over to drink, he saw another fawn exactly like him looking back.

"You always see yourself in the water," explained Thumper "it's called a reflection." There was always more for Bambi to learn.

"Hello, Bambi," said a voice. This time, it wasn't a reflection, it was a real little doe who smiled at him, Bambi was so surprised that he bounded up, but he also felt very shy. The doe wasn't. She introduced herself. "My name is Faline. I'm your cousin. Would you like to play with me?" she said as she ran off.

Bambi began running too, but in his excitement, he tripped and fell in the water. Faline helped him to get up. Both of them were playing when they saw two does coming in their direction.

"Look Bambi, look who's coming," Faline said.

Bambi's mother, and another doe that Bambi didn't know, were approaching.

"That's my mother" Faline added "and she is your aunt."

Soon Bambi and Faline were playing happily together, chasing each other round the hills, hiding in bushes or behind trees. Every day they played new games. The whole forest was like a wonderful park for them and they only stopped playing at night. Bambi and Faline were always together and Thumper was a bit jealous.

"Your cousin is a sissy," he said one day, "she never wants to play with me."

"No she isn't," said Bambi "besides if you ate less clover, your belly wouldn't be so fat and you'd run faster, then you could play with us."

One day Bambi and Faline went with their mothers to a clearing where several deer had gathered. "Who are they waiting for?" asked Bambi.

"They are waiting for the King of the forest, the big stag. You will be the happiest and the proudest of all," said his mother.

"Why?" asked Bambi again, very impressed. "The big stag is your father and that's why everybody calls you little prince," answered his mother.

Then came the sound of pounding hooves and the big stag burst out of the woods.

Very scared, Bambi drew closer to his mother. The King was strong and beautiful and looked tenderly at his son.

"You must promise to be courageous and one day when I'm old you will, in your turn, become the King of the forest," the big stag told Bambi.

Life continued happily for
Bambi and his mother for
quite some time.

But one day it wasn't the
sun that awoke Bambi.

A frightening noise could
be heard all over the forest.
It was the sound of shooting.

"Danger, man!" cried the running deer. All the animals and birds fled into the trees. In just a moment the whole place looked deserted.

Bambi's mother began to run, crying "Bambi, hurry, hurry." The shooting seemed to get closer every minute.

"Why are men so mean?" Bambi thought. He ran as fast as he could, but his legs were getting tired. "Faster Bambi, faster," shouted his mother as they were fleeing.

It seemed as if their happy life had turned into a nightmare. Every shadow, every tree looked threatening. Suddenly just in front of Bambi and his mother, the big stag appeared.

"Follow me," he said, and he took them to a thicket. They heard the shouts and loud roaring noise go by, then everything was quiet again.

"You're safe now, my son," said the King, as he continued majestically on his way.

Bambi and his mother waited in the clearing until they were sure the hunters had gone away, then they returned to their home in the heart of the forest.

Soon summer was over and the weather grew colder. One morning Bambi woke up shivering to find that the world had turned white during the night.

Every blade of grass was covered with a white coat and so was every tree and every bush. His mother was watching him and said "That's snow, Bambi." Bambi put one hoof out onto the snow to test the cold crisp surface. Then he walked forward carefully lifting his feet high. It was a lovely winter's day and the sun sparkled on the snow.

In the distance, Bambi was surprised to see Thumper playing on top of the pond. He hurried towards his friend and skidded on the smooth slippery ice. Down he fell, as Thumper laughed.

Soon Bambi could walk on ice without slipping and he and Thumper had a fine time playing in the sun.

Once when they heard a faint snore from a snowbank, they looked down a deep burrow and saw the little skunk there, fast asleep.

"Let's wake him up," said Bambi. "No, skunks always sleep right through the winter," Thumper explained. "It's called hibernating."

Winter was a lot of fun, but as time went on, there was less and less food. All the animals became hungry. The squirrel, being very wise, had stored a lot of food inside a tree and now he had nothing to worry about. Bambi had to learn to dig in the ground to look for plants or grass.

Nights were long and very cold and Bambi always hurried back to his mother to keep warm as soon as the sun set.

One day Bambi got lost. Not far away, he suddenly heard a big bang. He was very frightened and ran as far as he could. Then he stopped, his heart pounding. Everything was completely silent. He looked all around, then he began to call desperately for his mother. Silently, the great prince of the forest appeared at his side. "Your mother can never be with you again," he said quietly. "Now you must be brave and learn to walk alone." Then he left and Bambi was all alone for a while. Fortunately Faline and her mother found Bambi and took him to their part of the forest.

Time went by and little by little Bambi's sorrow
lessened. The snow started melting and one day there
was no more. Everything was brown and damp but
something was already beginning to change. The forest
was awakening from its long sleep. All the animals were
out, smelling and sniffing for the coming spring.

The long winter was finally over and everybody was peeking out. Flowers were blooming here and there and the trees were tipped with leaves and buds.

The spring sun shone on Bambi's coat as he walked along the forest paths. He carried his head proudly for now he had a fine set of antlers.

Bambi wasn't a fawn anymore, he had grown tall and strong and he won all the races.

"Woo-Woo-Woo," flutters Mr Owl, busily flapping his wings.

"What is all this hubbub?" he asks with a frown, "won't you let me sleep? It's been days since I slept a wink. Has everybody gone crazy?"

"Nobody is crazy, Mr Owl, it's springtime and we are all getting ready for the happy days ahead," said Thumper.

One day Bambi was walking alone in the forest and he began day-dreaming. He thought of his father and of his mother who was no longer with him. He remembered what his father had said to him and it seemed that things had changed. He wasn't a little fawn anymore, that he knew, but what was it that had changed? He couldn't tell.

Suddenly, he wasn't alone anymore. Standing next to him was a beautiful doe. "Do you remember me, Bambi?" she asked, "I'm Faline" and she licked his nose with her pink tongue. Both of them went on down the path together.

They were back together again running and jumping, but it wasn't the same as it used to be. Faline seemed to play with Bambi, but when he got closer, she ran away from him and then she waited for him a little distance away.

Bambi was really entranced by Faline. He didn't pay much attention to anything else because all that mattered was his pretty little cousin. Suddenly, one day as he was chasing Faline, in one of their endless games, Bambi understood what it was that had changed.

He was a tall and strong deer now, it was spring and most of all, he was in love.

Bambi ran to Faline, to tell her what he had discovered, but as he stood close to her, short of breath, he saw that she had known all along. "Faline," he began, anyway, "will you marry me? I promise to love you and to protect you as long as I live."

Faline didn't answer, but she held out her long and delicate paw.

"Not so fast," said a deep voice, "Faline is going with me."

It was Ronno, the deer, his antlers lowered ready for battle. "I don't want to fight," said Bambi, who hated fights, "I love Faline and she loves me, so we will get married." "That's exactly what I mean," said Ronno, "I want to marry Faline, so you must go away."

"Faline didn't choose you," Bambi pointed out, "she chose me. I'll fight for her if I must, but I do believe that you ought to be reasonable and understand the situation."

Instead of calming Ronno down, these words seemed to infuriate him even more. "The truth is that you're afraid to fight and that you are a coward," he said. Then Bambi was convinced that there was no alternative but to fight. He wasted no time and charged straight at Ronno. They met with a crash and fought fiercely until, at last, Bambi wounded Ronno in the shoulder.

By now Bambi's and Ronno's antlers had become entangled. Bambi heard Faline call him and he managed to free himself and hold his head up high with pride.

He knew that for Faline he could do anything.

While Ronno, beaten at last, was limping off into the forest, Bambi climbed up on a clifff and waited for Faline to join him. Now there was nothing to fear anymore.

Faline came back to Bambi's side and they walked away through the trees to the meadows to start their life together. Then one day the great stag came to Bambi saying, "Man is coming. I can hear dogs barking; it is man with tents and campfires. You must take care of yourself and Faline. We will have to go the hills."

News had spread quickly through the forest. All the animals were running back home and hiding.

Thumper, the rabbit, gathered his large family together.

The big stag was right: the sound of shooting was getting closer every minute. With hunter's shouts and dog's barks the whole forest was in turmoil. The dogs seemed to be everywhere. When Bambi left that morning to fetch some food, he showed Faline a steep cliff where she should hide in case of danger. "If I can't get back home, I'll be waiting for you there," Bambi explained reassuringly.

Later in the day, the shooting got even closer.

When Faline saw the dogs in the distance, she immediately started running and she didn't stop until she had reached the cliff. Bambi was already there waiting for her. "Hurry, Faline," he shouted, as he saw a dog very close behind her.

More dogs could be seen not far from the cliff. As Faline was climbing up, Bambi held the dog off with his antlers. He remembered what the big stag had said a long time ago, when he had seen him for the first time in the clearing, "Be brave," he had said. As he was defending Faline against the dog, Bambi could still hear the deep voice of his father saying "Be brave, Bambi." Yes, he must be brave; he must save Faline and himself.

Bambi and Faline galloped as fast and as far as they could and at last it seemed that the dogs had given up.

"Bambi, what is that red light over there?" Faline suddenly asked.

74

Fire, that's what it was. The forest was on fire from
the campfires. All the young trees were already
blackened. Suddenly they were surrounded by smoke
and Bambi couldn't see Faline. She didn't answer when
he called her. Bambi started to run and run again until
he reached a clearing. The great stag was there, Bambi
looked at his father with sadness.

"Where is Faline?" the great stag asked.

"We ran away from the dogs and I lost her in the smoke. I have been looking for her." Bambi answered.

"Hurry, son, we must make for the river."

Bambi had been wounded by the dog and he followed limping. He thought of how his mother must have suffered when she had been killed by the hunters. "If only I knew where Faline was!" Bambi sighed. "Come, son, this is no time for discouragement," the big stag said trying to cheer him up.

They rushed through the fire, through the cool water of the river and onto the far shore. Many other animals had already reached safety there.

To Bambi's great relief and joy, Faline was there too, and she gently licked Bambi's wounded shoulder.

"Safe at last!" Bambi exclaimed and it seemed all his troubles were forgotten now that he was with Faline again.

When they were able to go back to where they once lived, everything was black and bare; no leaves, no flowers, no grass. "We will have to look for another place," Bambi said sadly.

"It doesn't matter, Bambi, we are alive, that's all that counts," Faline said. Both of them went to look for their friends, Thumper, the rabbit, and his family, Mr Owl and the squirrel. By nightfall, they had found everybody and once again felt safe and secure.

Winter went by and the fire-blackened forest came to life again.

By spring time new leaves and flowers grew and grass covered everything. No-one could tell that there had been a fire and the forest was beautiful again. The mole and all her baby moles poked their heads out of the ground, but the sun was too bright for them. "We'll wait until the sun sets," said the mother and they all slipped back into their hole.

The sun felt nice and warm.

The squirrel yawned and stretched. He was anxious to jump and somersault in the trees again after the long winter's sleep. Just as he was getting ready to leap, Thumper the rabbit arrived. "Have you heard the news? Faline has had two babies! Let's go and see them."

Most of the animals had already left to go and admire Faline and Bambi's new-born fawns.

"I'm following you," the squirrel said and off they went. Thumper had already announced the good news to all the animals and they were rushing from every corner of the forest. As usual, Mr Owl was dozing on a branch. "Wake up, Owl, it's no time to sleep," Thumper shouted when he saw him still gently rocking in his sleep. "What, what is it?" said Mr Owl who almost fell out of the tree after being so suddenly awakened. "It's you again, you little rascal! Won't you ever let me sleep!"

Mr Owl was very angry, but Thumper couldn't care less. "Listen to the good news, owl, Bambi just had babies!"

As they drew closer to the thicket where Faline and Bambi lived, the animals lowered their voices.

"Shhh, don't make so much noise, you'll wake up the babies!" whispered Thumper. "Here they are, look at them!" The new-born princes of the forest were sleeping like Bambi did once upon a time, long ago.

"Congratulations Faline," said Mr Owl, bowing.

"Thank you all for coming," said Faline "but we must let them sleep. They are very small."

"I know a lullaby." Thumper said. "I don't think it's necessary, look they're fast asleep." Faline replied. Thumper was a little disappointed, but Faline told him to come back tomorrow.

Not far away the proud father Bambi watched over his family. The next day, the little fawns opened their eyes and made their first attempts to stand up. Soon they were able to walk. All the animals had come back to see them now that they were wide awake.

Startled by the crowd, the fawns snuggled against each other. "Don't be afraid, they're all your friends," said Faline "and they've come to say hello."

Bambi now was the head of a family. He had to fetch food for them and make sure that everything was quiet and safe.

One day as he reached a clearing he saw his father, the great stag, emerge from the forest. He came over to Bambi and said "I'm happy for you and Faline. You'll be good parents and bring up your children as well as your mother and I did." Bambi saw that the majestic antlers of his father had grown even bigger and more beautiful since last time he had seen him. He was so proud to be the son of the king of the forest.

"My son," the stag began "I've waited a long time for this day to come. Thanks to you and Faline, there will be more little fawns in the forest. They will become grown-up deer themselves and have fawns, too.

That is the way it should be. Now it is time for me to let you take my place. You've become a strong and experienced deer. Everybody in the forest loves you and respects you. It is your turn to become the king of the forest."

"No, that can't be," Bambi whispered, "you are the king and you will remain the king."

"No, Bambi," said the big stag, "everything comes to an end. I've grown old and one cannot be the king anymore when one isn't strong enough. You are the one who is strong enough now and wise also. I give over my kingdom to you. I know you will be a good king. When you feel tired or sad, think of me and of your mother."

The big stag left then and Bambi saw him disappear into the forest, just as he had appeared the first time, years ago, when Bambi was still a little fawn.

As Bambi went back to Faline, he thought to himself that she was a queen now and that his babies were princes and princesses. He felt proud and happy. "Faline," he said when he got back to her, "I am the king of the forest, and we will always be together." Faline gently put her paw on his, she didn't need to say anything.

This edition produced exclusively for
Longmeadow Press
by Twin Books

ISBN 0-681-40108-7

Printed in Hong Kong